For Zenna

Bloomsbury Publishing, London, Oxford, New York, New Delhi and Sydney

First published in Great Britain in June 2019 by Bloomsbury Publishing Plc
50 Bedford Square, London WC1B 3DP

First published in the USA in June 2019 by Bloomsbury Children's Books
1385 Broadway, New York, New York 10018

www.bloomsbury.com

BLOOMSBURY is a registered trademark of Bloomsbury Publishing Plc

Text and illustrations © Jacob Grant 2019

The moral rights of the author and illustrator have been asserted

A CIP catalogue record of this book is available from the British Library

ISBN 978 1 5266 0741 6

All papers used by Bloomsbury Publishing are natural, recyclable products made
from wood grown in well-managed forests. The manufacturing processes
conform to the environmental regulations of the country of origin

Printed and bound in China by Leo Paper Products

1 3 5 7 9 10 8 6 4 2

Bear Out There

JACOB GRANT

BLOOMSBURY
CHILDREN'S BOOKS
LONDON OXFORD NEW YORK NEW DELHI SYDNEY

Spider had made a kite.
He was very excited to fly it out in the garden.

Spider loved the outdoors.
He liked the warm sun.
He liked the fresh breeze.
He liked the colourful plants all around.

The bugs were also nice.

His friend Bear did not agree.

"Who would want to go outside when there
are so many fun things to do inside?"

Bear had planned a tidy day at the house,
followed by a nice cup of tea in his cosy chair.

But plans have a way of changing.

"Spider, you are my friend, so I'll help you find your kite," said Bear. "But you know I do *not* like the forest."

Bear did not like the dirty ground.
He did not like the itchy plants.
He did not like the pesky bugs all around.

Spider thought a search in the forest could be fun.

Then Bear began to grumble.

"Who would want to smell so many yucky weeds?" said Bear.

"Who would want to hear all this noisy twitter?"

"Who would ever want to see
such a horrid forest?"

The two friends walked on,
and still they could not find the kite.

Spider no longer thought the search
was much fun either.

The cold rain made Bear grumble
more than ever.

"What a mess!" he said. "This search
can't get any worse!"

But it could.

Bear did not grumble any more.
Bear did not do anything at all.
Bear was done.

They had tried to find Spider's kite,
and they had failed.

"I am going home to my cosy chair
and a nice cup of tea," said Bear.

Bear paused for a long moment.

"Maybe we could look just a *little* further."

Even if they could not find the kite, Spider was happy to have his friend with him.

"We have not had much luck on our walk," said Bear. "But at least the rain is stopping. Look!"

When Spider and Bear looked up,
they saw more than clouds.

Back at home, the two friends patched up Spider's kite. And they even made something special for Bear.

"Now, who wants to relax with a nice cup of tea?" asked Bear.